Taos Pueblo

Philip Reno

Introduction by John Collier

Second Revised Edition

SAGE BOOKS

THE SWALLOW PRESS INC.
CHICAGO

Copyright © 1963, 1972 by Philip Reno
All rights reserved
Printed in the United States of America

Second Edition
   First Printing

Sage Books are published by
The Swallow Press Incorporated
1139 South Wabash Avenue
Chicago, Illinois 60605

This book is printed on 100% recycled paper

ISBN 0-8040-0329-7
Library of Congress Catalog Card Number 72-78538

No Feeble Will

John Collier

I first came to Taos in 1920, my family and myself the guests of Antonio and Mabel Luhan. Just at this time, starting in fact in 1921, the Interior Department, under Albert Fall, and the Indian Bureau had launched a campaign to destroy the Pueblos physically and spiritually. And against this destroying intention and fact the Pueblos rose as one man; they reformed the all-Pueblo organization which had driven Spain from New Granada in 1680. But the battle the Pueblos waged after 1922 was for public opinion, a battle in Congress and in the courts.

Waged with perseverance and unanimity and with dramatic and political skill, this united Pueblo effort across twelve years saved the Pueblos, and laid the foundation for the Indian New Deal and the Indian Reorganization Act — for fundamental changes in the United States policy toward all United States Indians.

So many times, in so many ways, across fifteen hundred years, the Pueblos have seemed barely poised at the edge of destruction; have seemed, even, to be pushed over the edge by that fearful contingency which, in world history and in our present hour, we experience as almost universal fate. Out of many such crises in Pueblo life, I mention two that preceded the assaults of the 1920's mentioned above.

The first of these crises came with the ending of the Pueblo epoch which archeologists term "Classic Pueblo." Commencing about 1000 A.D., Pueblo clan organizations numbering many hundreds had united to build and to administer true cities, with populations of thousands in each. Their agriculture, craft techniques, languages, and vast ceremonial systems, which had developed across more than a thousand years, entered on a marvelous efflorescence at the Mesa Verde cliff-cities, at Aztec and Casa Grande, and variously in what is now the "Four Corners" area.

Then, in 1276 A.D., the Great Drought commenced. It lasted twenty-three years. Herbiage was dessicated, game retreated to distant mountains or perished, flood-water farming became impossible, even drinking water disappeared. The nomad tribes (Navajos, Utes, and Apaches), themselves desperate from the drought, raided the diminished corn fields by night. And within the Great Drought, none could foretell its end.

Every one of the great Classic Pueblo cities was silently abandoned, abandoned forever. The clans which had built and administered the cities drifted away – some to the Hopi country, some to the Zuñi Pueblo, some to the Rio Grande.

Two hundred and fifty silent years passed, and then Coronado with his army reached Zuñi and the Rio Grande country. With Coronado arrived Pedro de Casteñada, one of the great chroniclers of the Spanish New World. And Casteñada described the Pueblos as of 1541. Here cities had grown again, comparable to the cities of the Classic Pueblo time; cities compounded, as the Classic Pueblo cities had been, of numerous clans, with Pueblo-wide secret societies and with perfections of agriculture and of ceremony which filled Casteñada with wonder.

The second crisis came with the Spanish. Broadly speaking, Spain, between 1541 and 1600, destroyed the Pueblo great age which Casteñada had described. Under Spanish ferocity and greed, Spanish fanaticism against heathen religions, and the Spanish way of enslaving Indians, various Pueblo biological stocks became extinct. Every New Mexico Pueblo which survived did so by weaving around itself an impenetrable veil of secrecy which no white man could penetrate. Behind its impenetrable veil, each Pueblo controlled its own inner destiny, and each Pueblo dealt with the white world through an annually chosen secular government. That is the way it is now.

In all the Pueblo crises, as in the three mentioned above, assault from without has confronted the Pueblos with crises that had to be met by drawing on their inner powers, and has strengthened them, not weakened or effaced them. As to whether they will continue to survive – in ways of their ancient genius – I note two related circumstances of their genius. The first is that our Pueblos of New Mexico and Arizona are Ancient Man. "Anasazis" the Navajos named them, six centuries ago; the word means The People from of Old. The second thing to see and understand about the Indian genius is that in terms of the man-nature relationship, the ecological principle, the saving reverence for life, it is they, not we, who are "in the morning of the times."

Fourteen years ago, musing about whether the life river of the

Pueblos would again become a sunken river, and even a river sunken forever, I came to the answer which would be my answer now:

"They (the Pueblos) have lived the dangerous life, have breasted tides of change, and not only since the white man came; they have incorporated change following upon change; and their continuity has not been broken, the inward and outward direction of their genius has not been altered.

"They are not inchoate societies, but subtly structured ones, and not petrified societies, but constantly developing, evolving ones, now as of old. They hold their profundities, but they are efficient and practical, too. They do not fear the world.

"In truth, no man can give the answer that these Indians in their institutions and spirit shall or shall not go on. No man can answer another question now: Shall human society and the human spirit go on... There are words quoted by Poe in Lygeia, from an ancient source.

" 'Man does not yield himself to the angels, or to death utterly, save through the weakness of his own feeble will.'

"No feeble will is that of the Indians of the American Southwest."

Taos cacique Juan de Jesus Romero and interpreter Paul Bernal testifying for the return of Blue Lake to Pueblo ownership. A member of the cacique's family and Pueblo officials are beside him. *Photo courtesy of Northern Pueblos Agency, B.I.A.*

North Pueblo of Taos, sacred mountain in the background. *Photo courtesy of the Museum of New Mexico collections.*

Taos Indian History

Taos Indians know their history through two sources — through the ceremonies, songs and legends taught by tribal elders to each generation and also through scholarly studies. Some of the studies have been made by Indian scholars, and Indians have contributed to nearly all. Non-Indians know of Indian history through these studies, and through tribal accounts and stories whose content is not religious and which may therefore be shared with outsiders.

A thousand years before white men arrived Indians were building early Pueblo villages along the Rio Grande River and up and down the small streams that fed it. By A.D. 900 small pueblos had developed in the Taos area, along with agricultural technology capable of supporting village life. Beginning about the year 1200 Rio Grande Valley Indians built large adobe Pueblos. Taos Pueblo was built sometime between 1300 and 1400.

Technology for erection of the Taos Pueblo buildings may have been brought by Indians from Chaco Canyon and Mesa Verde, displaced by the great drought that devastated those areas in the late 1200's. Indians from Chaco Canyon in particular may have made their way to the upper Rio Grande valleys, sharing the valley lands and game with Indians already living there and bringing advanced technology and its facilitating ritual.

By the time that Taos Pueblo was built Indian settlement had extended to every side of Taos valley. Remnants of pueblo walls and mounds which cover pit houses disclose villages in which Indians lived on the western side of Ranchos de Taos valley, where Llano Quemado is now, and near the hot springs above Llano. Petroglyphs and pictographs tell of Indian ceremonial grounds near Los Cordovas, and ruins of Indian dwellings dot the sunward slopes of Valdez and Hondo valleys north of Taos. There is almost no field or sagebrush tract where potsherds, arrowheads and stone tools left from ancient homes and abandoned campsites may be found.

Some Indian people moved up the Ranchos valley to a place that later Spanish-speaking people name for potsherds they found above pit houses there. By then the Indians had long since left El Rito de Las Ollas, or Pot Creek, and moved on to found Picuris Pueblo. The Picuris Indians today speak a language similar to that of Taos and follow many similar customs. Other Indian tribes related to the Taos and Picuris include those of Sandia and Isleta Pueblos. The language spoken by these related tribes is Tiwa, a branch of the Tanoan language group which also includes the Tewa and Towa Pueblo Indian languages.

The name Taos is apparently the Spanish plural — adding an s — of the Taos Indian name for themselves. Tao is a common family word in the various Tanoan languages, meaning to dwell, or house or pueblo. Another Taos name for their Pueblo is Ialaphai, meaning red willow trees. The earliest Spanish chroniclers called the village Braba, or Yuraba, but by the time of Onate's journal in 1598 the village was called Taos, as it has been ever since.

The ancestors of the Taos Indians probably came from Asia, crossing over a land bridge that spanned or nearly spanned the Bering Strait near the end of the last ice age. For ten thousand years or more migrations of people of different racial stocks, languages, cultures and technologies followed game across this land bridge from Asia to the new world. South they moved, still following herds of game, down the corridor between the ice fields of western Canada, and on along the eastern slopes of the Rocky Mountains. Spreading out as they moved south, Indians had, long before the white men came, occupied every corner of the Americas.

With them from Asia they brought fire, stone tools, domesticated dogs, and language. However, no Indian language that we know of can be traced to any language found in Asia today, and the rich and diffuse Indian languages must have been developed in this hemisphere. So must plants which now provide more than half the hemisphere's agricultural wealth. Corn is the most important of these crops, and its creation from wild grasses must have been the most complex, for it cannot sow itself or take care of itself. But corn is only one of more than twenty crops that were developed from wild growth by Indians in this hemisphere; these included pineapples, strawberries, peanuts, beans, squash, pumpkins, chocolate, and tobacco.

Some people think that the scientific knowledge of the American Indians was brought to them by Chinese who sailed ships across the

Pacific many centuries after the northern migration routes had been blocked by sea and ice. Seeking a tie between ancient Chinese and the American Indians has been an ardent endeavor of many who long for a deeper meaning in life than their materialist ambient offers them. Most United States scholars believe, however, that all the Mayan, Toltec, Inca, and other Indian astronomy, mathematics, agriculture, and art were products of this hemisphere. Latin American Indian scholars put more stock in evidence linking pre-Columbian American Indians with Asian technologies and cultures.

Long after the last Indian migrations from Asia, the first wave of white immigration rolled over Middle and South America, decimating the Indian populations and devastating their cultures. A Spanish force led by Alvarado reached Taos in 1540, but Taos was a remote outpost of the Spanish empire, and the Pueblo survived Spanish rule relatively unscathed.

The second great wave of white immigrants followed nearly 300 years after the first, and like the first swept across America seeking gold and land. This wave of immigrants reached Taos shortly before the middle of the nineteenth century. Both waves brought storm and strife to the peoples they engulfed. Later chapters of this brief account summarize the ways in which Taos Indians coped with these successive threats to their culture and their land.

Winter is a quiet time at Taos Pueblo. Six weeks before and after the winter solstice are kept free of intrusions by motors on Pueblo life. *Photo courtesy of Mildred T. Crews.*

Pueblo Government

Taos Pueblo has always been and is today, in common with most Indian tribes, a self-governing community, compared by some scholars to the city-states of ancient Greece. The analogy is limited, of course, one of the various significant differences being the important role that women play in Pueblo community life.

The Pueblo vests civil authority in officers elected at the beginning of each year. The Governor of the Pueblo is its executive officer and its spokesman. He is assisted by a Lieutenant Governer, and by officers also selected each new year. From the time the Governor is elected, he carries two canes which signify authority. One of these canes was given to the Pueblo by King Charles V of Spain. The other was given by President Lincoln, who called the Pueblo Governors to Washington and presented them with patents to the Pueblo lands as well as with the canes. Among those also assisting the Governor is the Tribal Interpreter. In all meetings outside the Pueblo or with visitors or officials from outside the Pueblo, the Interpreter translates the Governor's words into English and Spanish, and translates to the Governor the words of the people he is meeting with.

A War Chief is also elected each year to be responsible for "foreign relations" – that is, for dealing with matters coming up from outside the Pueblo. It may seem odd to keep this title now, unless we remember that among Indians it always was the War Chief's duty to preserve the spiritual fitness of the tribe, rather than simply to prepare for and wage war, as in some other cultures we know fairly well.

Among the War Chief's duties are relations between the Forest Service and the Taos Indian firefighting crews. This is why the cabinet of firefighting tools stands each year beside the War Chief's door. Indian firefighters are trained by the Forest Service and are flown to put out forest fires everywhere in the West. Taos firefighting crews have been called the "Snowballs" ever since a heavy snow started falling on them just as they were cleaning up a fire in the Lincoln National Forest.

Former Taos Pueblo Governor Seferino Martinez, who led his people's efforts for their sacred Blue Lake area.

Tribal policies and questions are decided by the Pueblo Council on which serve the tribe's civil officers and the leaders of the tribal organizations. The Council carries on its business in a manner as democratic as any in the world. It meets as often as necessary and deliberates until the question it is taking up has been looked at from all directions. Council decisions usually proceed from general agreement rather than from a simple majority vote and lack of unanimous consent may hold up any action until all are in agreement. The result is sometimes a delay that is incomprehensible to white outsiders to whom agreement and understanding are less important than action and change.

The men who make up the Tribal Council have longstanding experience in tribal affairs, and lifelong education in tribal belief, so that they can make decisions in the spirit of the history and the future of the tribe. In the Council functions the Pueblo's civil government is joined with its religious and ceremonial life.

Behind the civil government, and above it, stand the Pueblo's ancient social forms, founded in the Pueblo's religion and way of life. Indian life is integrated through religion, the gods walk on every road of life. And believing that life's meaning is universal, Indians do not believe in competition between one religion and another, but welcome all beliefs. Most Taos Indians are Catholics, and have been for several hundred years.

Chief ceremonial officer of the Pueblo is the cacique, which is an hereditary office. The cacique trains throughout his youth, holds office for life, and devotes all his time to his duties. (The word "cacique" was brought to the Southwest by the Spanish, who took it from the French word used in Haiti to mean tribal chief.) Associated with the cacique in ceremonial work are the kiva chiefs. There are six kivas, the ceremonial societies' halls or meeting rooms, corresponding to the six directions — north, east, south, west, up, and down. Tribal education and training are carried on through the kivas, as well as the expression of tribal religious life.

Pueblo Buildings

Taos Pueblo itself was founded, legend has it, in the language of legends, by a great chief who, following an eagle, led his people up a sparkling stream to the foot of the mountains. Where the eagle dropped two plumes, one falling on either side of the stream, the Indians built their permanent home.

The Pueblo was built of adobe, but not of adobe bricks as today's practice is. Large sections of mud were compacted into place, so that the walls were even thicker than those built now. As is true today, log vigas supported the roof which was made of poles and branches covered with grass and earth, and the walls were plastered with adobe mud. The entrance to each apartment was through the roof, for safety's sake. Pole ladders which could be pulled up furnished the usual access to the roof. The circular ovens used in the Pueblo for baking bread were probably introduced by the Spanish. They resemble closely the ovens the Moors brought to Spain from Africa.

Adobe buildings need to be cared for conscientiously or they weather and disintegrate as rain and ground water reaches them. The mud and straw plaster must be renewed regularly, the roofs of earth patched and compacted and drainage checked, deteriorating adobes replaced, and old beams and boards scrutinized. Much of this work is done by family groups, and major work is often done communally. The plastering is of special interest, the women applying the mud, forming and smoothing it, traditionally working it with a sheepskin to give it a final finish.

All Taos Indians who live in the Pueblo, regardless of position or economic means, take part in community work to repair the Pueblo structures, to keep the village clean, to ready the irrigation ditches, and to care for community property.

The only indigenous architecture of the United States is found in the Pueblos, and a school of Southwest architecture has developed from the pueblo structural qualities and design. Besides homes and communities that follow the pueblo forms, a general concept has grown up called "Modern Pueblo" by an architect noted particularly for developing this concept in the buildings of the University of New Mexico. This concept is one of massive walls rising to various levels, from which rise further elevations in receding natural rhythms. The charm and distinction of this form is clearly derived from Taos Pueblo.

"The architecture of the Pueblos is dignified," Alida Sims wrote as long ago as 1922, "of definite type, a complete expression of the needs of the Indian and of the material at hand. It is elemental in its simplicity, sculptural in quality, whether the walls be smooth or rough, and with enough variety in detail to make it structurally interesting."

Indians wear blankets to keep themselves warm in winter, and they say, cool in summer. As in all Indian customs, tradition is bound to practicality as well as to legend and belief. *Photo courtesy of the Museum of New Mexico collections.*

Pueblo architecture: "Massive walls rising to various levels, from which rise further elevations in receding natural rhythms." *Photo courtesy of New Mexico Department of Development.*

Horses and wagons are still used for work as well as for pleasure at the Pueblo. *Photo courtesy of New Mexico Department of Development.*

Taos Indian dancers keep alive the traditional songs and dances and integrate them with new variations. Pueblo Indian costumes share many colorful features with costumes of Indians of Mexico, including feathers of tropical birds. *Photo courtesy of New Mexico Department of Development.*

Songs, Dances and Ceremonies

Taos Pueblo ceremonies are held on various occasions throughout the year, in time with changing seasons, growing crops and harvests, and the general rhythms of living things. Songs and dances are integrated with religious ritual in the ceremonies, and are often performed in the Pueblo plaza where visitors are welcome. Photos are not permitted of these dances, however. Visitors should be sure to ask the Pueblo officer at the plaza entrance before taking any photos. A permit can be obtained for taking photos of nonreligious places and events.

The ceremonies are carefully prepared for and the color and beauty of the costumes, the precision of the dances and the rhythm of the formal choruses and chants reflect the meaning that the ceremonies have in the life of the people. Perhaps the best known of all is the Deer Dance, held each year either on Christmas or on January 6, Twelfth-day. In this dance the men wear the hides and horns of the deer they have taken in the fall hunting season. The dance is led by a "Deer Lady," carefully chosen by the spiritual leaders of the Pueblo. Many Indian tribes of our Southwest and of Mexico have long performed deer dances. All these dances have in common a kind of invocation to the deer, and a common symbolism, but each one is different in form and character from all the others. Of all these Indian deer dances, the Taos is the most massive and the most remote from white experience. It has a profound effect on many who see it and has been described in dozens of books and records.

Almost as well known as the Deer Dance is the Christmas Eve procession at the Pueblo. This procession, beginning from a Mass at sundown, is led through an avenue of blazing piñon farolitos by Indians firing rifles into the smoke-filled air. Drummers and dancers follow, and then blanketed Indians carrying the Virgin on a canopied platform. Many artists have painted the dramatic and moving scene, among them Taos artists Oscar Berninghaus, Dorothy Brett, Louis Ribak, Ila McAfee, Emil Bistram, and Charles Reynolds.

Some years the Matachines Dance is performed on Christmas rather than the Deer Dance. This dance was, it is generally believed, brought over to the New World from Spain soon after the Conquest, and followed the Spanish north into New Mexico. However, the Indian legend is that Montezuma himself brought the dance northward before the Spanish came, and taught it to the Rio Grande Pueblos. It is performed in many of these Pueblos at Christmas time and, in a somewhat different form, by Indians of Mexico.

The Turtle Dance is a serene and lovely dance given New Year's Day by the Turtle Clan. The Buffalo Dance is given January 6th when the Deer Dance is given Christmas Day. During the spring and summer are the dances known as corn dances.

The most sacred Taos ceremonies are held in late summer at Blue Lake, most sacred of all Taos Indian shrines. The Pueblo does not permit visitors at these ceremonies.

Because of its favorable location, Taos has for time immemorial been a meeting place and trading center for different tribes and races. The conclusion of summer harvests is everywhere a time for thanksgiving and celebration, and the Taos Pueblo fall fiesta is held on September 30th, the day of San Geronimo, the Pueblo's patron saint. Other tribes bring pottery, blankets, jewelry, melons, and chile to sell and trade, and everyone is welcomed to "take fiesta" in the homes of friends. Relay races open the San Geronimo fiesta early in the morning, and also the morning of El Dia de Santa Cruz, May 3rd.

Taos Indians have many songs and dances in addition to those that are religious and ceremonial. Round dances are a social dance in which visitors are often asked to take part. "Forty-niners" are recreational and social songs comprised of vocables (for example, "haya, haya, haya") and often humorous phrases and verses, "I'll take you home in my one-eyed Ford..."

Since religious songs and dances cannot be performed away from the Pueblo, Taos people composed new songs and dances for fiestas and "pow-wows" in other places. A number of Taos dance groups have been formed, and some of them win prizes regularly at occasions like the Gallup Ceremonial. The hoop dance, for example, is said to have been originated by Taos dancers at an Oklahoma pow-wow some 60 years ago. Costumes, music and steps of many of these secular dances — the War Dance and Shield Dance among others — show a strong Plains Indian influence, and a number are known as Comanche songs and dances.

San Geronimo Fiesta about fifty years ago. *Photo courtesy of the Museum of New Mexico collections.*

The drum is the basic Indian musical instrument and almost all singing is accompanied on a drum. An Indian flute, carved from cedar wood, is also played from time to time, often in solitude. Indian music is different in its rhythms from those of European cultures. Once Leopold Stokowski stayed in Taos to study Indian music, but he found that he could not set it down in the measures to which he was accustomed.

Ceremonial Occasions at Taos Pueblo

January 1	Turtle Dance
January 6	Buffalo Dance or Deer Dance
Early February	Feather, Hand and Belt Dances
Easter	Dances and ceremonies
May 3, (Santa Cruz)	Relay races, Corn Dances Children's and young people's dances
May 14 and 15 (San Isidro)	Blessing of fields
June 13 (San Antonio)	Corn Dances
June 24 (San Juan)	Rabbit hunt, Corn Dances
July 25 and 26 (Santa Ana and Santiago)	Town of Taos Fiesta, Pueblo participation
September 29 and 30 (San Geronimo)	Sunset Dances, pole climbing, Pueblo fiesta, various dances, Chifonetti
Christmas Eve	Procession
Christmas Day	Deer Dance or Matachines

Taos Pueblo Land

In times before the white man came and land turned into a source of strife and corruption, each Indian tribe held lands generally recognized as belonging to it. The lands which the Taos Indians held — on which they laid out their irrigation ditches and planted crops, built their homes and camps, and hunted game — were the valley of Taos and the mountains above the Pueblo. The boundaries of this land ran east from the Rio Grande River, up the Rio Hondo past Wheeler Peak, then south around Blue Lake, west down the mountain ridges back of the Pueblo, on past the Ranchos valley to the end of the Picuris mountain spur, then north along the Rio Grande to the Hondo canyon. This area of "aboriginal use and occupancy" amounted to about 300,000 acres, a small area for an Indian tribe of those times, but one which the Taos Indians used intensively.

When the Spanish first came to New Mexico, they lived at the Indian villages. Taos was one of the Pueblos which gave the Spanish food, shelter, and protection from warring tribes. As time went on a Spanish village named Don Fernando (or Fernandez) de Taos grew up where Taos is now. One story is that the Indians, alarmed at Spanish religious intrusion on Pueblo life, asked the Spanish to move a league away.

In general Spanish law accorded Pueblo Indians title to their land of original use and occupancy, except for particular tracts granted to others by the Spanish king. The kings gave particular grants of land throughout New Spain and New Granada to Spanish noblemen. To insure the Pueblo Indians against loss of their village lands, the kings gave each Pueblo a tract of land extending a league outward in each direction from the Pueblo church. A few Spanish grandees were given land in Taos valley and up the Rio Grande de Ranchos valley, but at the close of Spanish rule the Taos Indians' mountain area was intact and was recognized to be theirs under Spanish law. The Pueblo was also recognized to have prior water rights to all streams which crossed their land.

When Mexico won independence from Spain, the Mexican Declaration of Independence recognized the principle that "all inhabitants of New Spain without distinction, whether European, Africans, or Indians, are citizens... and that the person and property of every citizen will be respected by the government." Taos remained under jurisdiction of the Mexican government for a quarter of a century, until American troops — following American traders, trappers and prospectors — opened the American era in the Southwest. As the American era opened, Taos Pueblo had survived 250 years of Spanish and Mexican rule, successfully adjusting to the new environment and adopting new technologies. Pueblo mountain land was still intact as well as the upper half of Pueblo valley land. The lower half had been taken by Spanish settlers.

The American conquest of the northern half of Mexico, including New Mexico, was part of the great American westward expansion that reduced American Indian land to a relatively few acres that whites did not want. As President Cleveland remarked about a congressional bill opening the way to white appropriation of Indian land, "the hunger and thirst of the white man for the Indian's land is almost equal to his hunger and thirst after righteousness." He nevertheless signed the bill.

Pueblo Indian land grants were apparently protected from white appropriation by terms of the Treaty of Guadalupe Hidalgo. Land beyond the Taos Pueblo grant boundaries, however, land which the Indians had always considered theirs and which was theirs under Spanish law, seemed open for white appropriation. The Pueblo's remaining valley land beyond the Pueblo grant boundaries was taken by whites, and in the early 1900's the mountain area back of Taos Pueblo was incorporated into the United States Forests. This area contains Blue Lake and a number of other Indian shrines.

In testimony before Congress, Pueblo Governor Seferino Martinez explained the meaning of the Blue Lake area. "Blue Lake is the most important of all our shrines because it is a part of our life, it is our Indian church. We go there for good reason, like any other people would go to their denomination. Different people go visit and give their humble word to God in any language that they speak. It is the same principle at Blue Lake. We go there and talk to our Great Spirit in our own language, and talk to nature and what is going to grow, and ask God Almighty, like anyone else would do."

Taos Pueblo was not consulted officially about the National Forest action taking over the Blue Lake area. Indians were given to understand, however, that Pueblo use of the area would be preserved, that Pueblo religious rites would be respected, and that the Forest Service would protect the area from commercial exploitation. By 1911 the Taos Indians were convinced that the promises were vainly given, "White man's promises." They began trying to get back their sacred area.

Taos Pueblo's struggle to regain its sacred land is one of America's epic stories. The effort went on for two-thirds of a century, deepening until it became the focus of all Pueblo efforts, and widening until it enlisted the united efforts of Indian Tribes and of a far reaching circle of Indian friends. Through all those years the Taos Indians rallied as one man to defend the tribal shrines. From the 1920's through the 1960's they mobilized, from the scarce resources of people living almost at the margin of subsistence, finances for court actions that ran on for years, for journeys to Washington, for appeals to white audiences to support their cause. Their land became a symbol of survival, so that in Taos the folk story grew that on the day when the Pueblo lost its land, or sold it, on that day the world would end.

Time and again the Indians thought they had won back their land — first in the Pueblo Lands Act and Lands Board decision of the mid-1920's, again in the Congressional Act of 1928, withdrawing the Blue Lake area from "entry or appropriation," and yet again in the Congressional Act of 1934, giving Taos Pueblo "exclusive use rights" to the area. Each victory was first corroded by interpretation and then broken down by practice of the entrenched bureaucracies and private white interests.

After World War II commercial interests turned increasingly to exploitation of the country's remaining wilderness areas, and pressures on the Blue Lake area mounted year by year. Tourist businesses demanded entry and the Forest Service laid out trails to the lake and camp grounds above it. Forest grazing permits closed in to the south of the area and mining interests closed in on the north. Timber interests built roads up from Eagle's Nest to the east.

As the 1950's were beginning, the Pueblo brought suit in the Indian Court of Claims for restoration of their land. In 1965 the Court finally handed down their decision, a decision which was a complete vindication of the Indian cause. The Indians' right to their land or original use and occupancy was upheld. The government had taken their land wrongfully — illegally in fact.

The Court could not return the land, however, it could only determine money damages. The Pueblo wanted their sacred land, not money for it. Congressional action was needed to return the land. The focus of the Taos endeavor turned to Congress.

In 1968 the House of Representatives passed a bill which Representative Haley sponsored to return the Indian land. Forest Service and recreation interests mobilized against the bill and it was buried in the Senate. In 1971 the House again passed Representative Haley's bill, and public opinion rallied overwhelmingly to the Indians. Senators McGovern, Harris and others supported the bill in the Senate, and President Nixon's endorsement finally sent it through to passage.

The long, long campaign was over. Taos Pueblo began to assemble conservation and fire fighting crews and to clear away the last obstacles to preservation of the land as a shrine of wilderness in a land coming, albeit belatedly, to appreciate the Indian concept of the relationship of land and life. In Frank Waters' words, "their Pueblo land is the Indian's universe in miniature, a center of his religion and belief, of his strength to live, and to understand and enjoy life."

Blue Lake in mid-summer.

Making a Living

Contrary to a mistaken belief widely held, the federal government makes no payments to individual Indians, who must make their living just as anyone else. Indians pay the same income, sales, and other taxes and are subject to the same laws as any citizen. In recognition of their record in the First World War, Indians were made citizens by Congress in 1924. New Mexico and a few other states did not give Indians living on reservations the right to vote until many years later, but now Indians have the same franchise rights as any citizen. Indian land is held in trust title by the federal government, however, and is not subject to state and local property taxes.

When the Spanish reached the Pueblo valleys, the Taos economy was essentially subsistence agriculture supplemented by hunting and by gathering wild crops. As the Spanish moved onto Pueblo land, new technology from Spain helped offset Taos Pueblo's smaller land base. Game was increasingly hard to find, but the Indians had taken on Spanish stock and Spanish stock-raising practices, and horses made longer hunting expeditions possible. Wheat and other crops introduced from Spain and Mexico added to agricultural production, and trade supplemented both food and technology.

Taos had always been a contact point between Pueblo and Plains Indians, and as time went on harvest fairs at Taos Pueblo became widely attended economic and social functions. Utes and Comanches came bringing captives to barter off, buckskins, buffalo hides, horses, guns, ammunition, knives and meat. Navajos brought horses, sheep and firewood; Pueblos brought food and handicrafts; Apaches came with skins and baskets.

American trappers and other "mountain men" were showing up in Taos by the 1830's, giving an added if uncouth zest to the fairs, and to life in Taos generally. Soon American traders were bringing new goods — tools, utensils, cloth, guns and moonshine whiskey — to add to the traditional goods bartered and sold in Taos.

Baking bread in a Pueblo oven, or horno. A fire is built in the oven, and when the oven is heated through and through the coals are taken out, the loaves are put in to bake, and the opening covered. *Photo courtesy of New Mexico Department of Development.*

Taos women use the Pueblo roof tops for drying corn and other crops and for curing jerky, thin strips of venison taken by the men in the fall hunting season. *Photo courtesy of Museum of New Mexico collections.*

In 1921 when John Collier came to visit Taos and stayed to take up the Indian cause, he was handed a government report which estimated the average income of Taos Indians to be less than $20 a year. Subsistence agriculture was still the economic base of Pueblo life, a lower level of subsistence in nutritional respects than before the white man had arrived.

Principal crops were corn and wheat, with some squash, oats, beans, peas, and melons, just as had been the case in 1896, according to a thesis written then about the Pueblo. Wheat was cut by sickle, and was threshed by goats and horses trampling it on a hardened adobe floor. The American plow had been in common use in 1896, and by 1922 these plows were pulled almost wholly by horses. In 1896, oxen had shared the task. Cash was replacing trader credit in 1896, and this was farther along by 1922, although $20 a year was even then an unlikely hallmark of a money economy. Before many years the American agricultural crisis of the 1920's, coupled with the revolution in transport technology, put an end to wheat farming in Taos. The mills and granaries stood empty for a long time, until one finally burned and others were put to social use, one becoming a jail.

Today the people are far from rich (their median annual income is less than $1000 *a family*), but they are in the money economy – the same money economy as the surrounding area. They buy their clothes, most of their food, their tools, services, transportation, and almost all their material needs.

The Pueblo economy is still primarily agricultural, with crops grown primarily to provide for the families that raise them, rather than for sale. Some hay is sold, but more is fed to Pueblo livestock. Some of the blue and red and multi-colored corn is sold in "ristras" to tourists and townspeople, and some is traded at Indian fairs for chile and mutton and other needed things. The best enchiladas in the world are made, everyone agrees, from blue corn meal. Fruit and truck crops are grown and traded for other goods, and chokecherries and Indian plums are picked and sold, but for the most part these crops are used by the families that raise and harvest them.

The fields that the Pueblo families farm were, in general, allotted to them by the tribe in earlier times, and passed down to children and relatives. Much of the Pueblo land is used communally for pasturing livestock belonging to the various families. The Pueblo Council has steadily used its community funds to buy land for grazing livestock, and in cooperation with the Soil Conservation Service has drilled wells and ploughed up sagebrush to plant dry-land grasses.

Cattle are the most numerous livestock and the Pueblo's most valuable agricultural product. A small herd of buffalo is kept for ceremonial reasons. There are some sheep, goats and pigs, but next to cattle the most numerous livestock is horses. The horses no longer serve much economic purpose, and the chord that horses strike in the Indian soul does not echo in the souls of agricultural experts and other government advisers. However, the increasing mechanization of the world enhances to the Indian the non-economic values that his horses have.

Taos Indians generally earn their living by working for wages as well as raising crops. Many are highly skilled in trades and crafts, but work is none too plentiful in Taos. During the 1950's the federal government put a lot of money and effort into a program to "relocate" Indians away from their homes and into cities. During the war able Indians had proved to learn skills very rapidly and to be conscientious and efficient workers. But few of the Indians ever felt at home in the cities. The Pueblo men and women still drummed and sang at the Indian centers set up there, but the songs of Zion ring uncertainly if they ring at all in strange lands. Especially as they married and their children began to grow up, the family ties and mutual aid and the tribal associations became too strong to resist. Before long they "relocated" themselves, this time back home from the cities.

Now that the Blue Lake issue is resolved, the Pueblo is turning to the solution of problems of livelihood and economic development. Electricity has been accepted at last. An Arts and Crafts cooperative is flourishing. A feasibility study has been made of tourism facilities on Pueblo land at the high bridge over the Rio Grande.

Some Taos Indians have trained as artists, and many of their paintings may be seen in galleries in New Mexico and some in other states. Indian artists face, of course, the economic dilemma that artists generally confront. A number of Taos Pueblo artisans do silver jewelry and leather work for businessmen in Taos, Santa Fe and Albuquerque. Of peculiarly Taos handicrafts, two products are best known — moccasins and drums.

The moccasins are hand made, of deerskin. Drums are rawhide stretched over cottonwood or aspen boles hollowed out by hand. Taos drums are treasured by Indians for their resonance, and by Indians and non-Indians alike for their aesthetic appeal. Taos pottery is made of clay from a special place the Indians know of containing minute particles of mica which gleam on the pottery surface.

Taos Deer Dance, a painting by Dorothy Brett. *Photo courtesy of Manchester Gallery, Taos. Photo by Mildred Crews.*

New Mexico's Troubles

A few years ago the Pueblo contingent in Taos town's summer fiesta carried a sign reading "All New Mexico's troubles begin in Taos." Then the troubles were listed, beginning with Po-pe, and the great rebellion of 1680.

War for Independence
In 1680 a revolt, led from Taos by a San Juan medicine man named Po-pe, routed the Spanish and drove them all the way south to El Paso del Norte, which was then across the Rio Grande in Mexico. The only white left in what is now New Mexico were a few captives kept as slaves. This was, Frank Reeve says in his *History of New Mexico,* not so much a revolt as a war for independence. Not for another hundred years, until 1776, did another successful war for independence begin in the Americas.

The Pueblo Indians had met the Spanish in peace, and in response to Spanish professions of friendship had given food and shelter as proof of their own. But the friendship soon withered. Spanish garrisons collected tribute levied on the Indians, extorted for each Spanish soldier an *encomienda* of Indian land with Indian serfs to work it, and tried to suppress the Indian religion. Indian protest was put down in violence, the Indian leaders hung, and the rank and file whipped and imprisoned, or sent as slaves to Spanish mines in Mexico.

At last, under Po-pe's leadership, the Indians joined together in an alliance of more than sixty Pueblos, united on so broad a scale for the first time, and for the last time until the 1920's. Even the Apaches and the Navajos joined the alliance. The revolt was planned and kept in strictest secrecy throughout four years of preparation for war, over a territory covering 40,000 square miles of mountains and desert, among tribes of many different languages and customs, directed toward a simultaneous uprising at dawn of a given day.

As the day drew near, action was unified through a cord which messengers from the inter-tribal council brought each tribe. In the cord were tied as many knots as there were days until the revolt was to begin. Each day one knot was untied. When the last knot was reached, the uprising would begin.

The plan was betrayed just before the appointed day, and Indian runners carried word from one Pueblo to another to start the war at once. The revolt succeeded, and the Spanish, in spite of their arms and knowledge of warfare, were driven from Santa Fe and out of New Mexico. When twelve years later Don Diego de Vargas led the Spanish back, they came as settlers. They accepted the Indian religions, seeking accommodation with them, and they sought co-operation instead of slavery. Po-pe had died, and the inter-tribal council had no heart for further war. The Indians received the Spanish in the spirit which the Spanish offered, in a friendship that has lasted on through the present.

New Mexico's Indian Governor

In 1836 the Mexican President appointed Coronel Albino Perez as Territorial Governor of New Mexico. The appointment angered the leaders of New Mexican society, who were used to having one of their own number – a Baca or a Chavez or an Armijo – as governor. They soon contrived, therefore, to incite an uprising against unpopular measures, chiefly new taxes, sponsored by Governor Perez. Northern New Mexico had grievances of long standing against the territorial government, and revolt was easily stirred up there.

The revolt is said to have been organized in Taos, but once started, made its headquarters in Santa Cruz. Quite a number of Pueblo Indians joined their Spanish neighbors in the rebel army, which was led by General "Chopon" of Taos. This army soon defeated Governor Perez, who was given no support whatever by the New Mexican aristocrats of Santa Fe and Albuquerque. The leaders of the rebel army then called together a General Assembly of the influential citizens and village leaders of northern New Mexico.

The General Assembly met in the Governors Palace in Santa Fe and elected Jose Gonzales of Taos as Governor of New Mexico. Jose Gonzales' mother was a Taos Pueblo Indian, and his father was of half Indian blood. The Assembly members knew that Indian support was necessary if they were to be able to accomplish anything.

The Assembly then named a committee to draft a statement of the grievances of the people and to present it to the Mexican Government. This committee was composed of Padre Antonio Jose Martinez of Taos, Don Juan Jose Esquibel, Alcalde of Santa Cruz, and Manuel Armijo, who had spoken for the wealthy *Rio Abajo,* down river, families during the planning of the uprising.

Instead of staying to help the Assembly, Manuel Armijo quickly left Santa Fe and organized a revolt of the Rio Abajo leaders against the new government. In this revolt, the Rio Abajo forces were joined by troops from the Mexican garrison at Chihuahua. Before a month had passed, Armijo's army had driven the Jose Gonzales government from Santa Fe, and soon had captured and executed its leaders.

The historian R. E. Twitchell writes that Jose Gonzales went of his own accord to Armijo's camp and greeted him: "Companero [for they had been associates in the uprising against Governor Perez] I come to ask for guarantees for my people, that no imposition or taxation be placed upon them, and so I will keep the peace."

Armijo beckoned to his guards, and then turned to Father Martinez, who had, probably in the hope of ameliorating Armijo's actions, accompanied him from Santa Fe. "Confess the *genizaro* [a man partly of Indian parentage]," Armijo told the Padre, "so that I may give him five bullets." Thus ended the government of New Mexico by its northern village leaders, under a Taos Indian governor.

The 1848 Revolt

Manuel Armijo was not left undisturbed to enjoy the power he had obtained so deviously. His second term of office ended when he fled to Mexico to escape an United States army that had invaded New Mexico, and was moving on Santa Fe. Arriving in Santa Fe almost unopposed, General Kearney's Army of the West paused long enough to hold a victory celebration and install Charles Bent as United States Territorial Governor of New Mexico. Kearney then went on post haste to California. He had heard that British warships were nearing the Pacific coast, and was afraid that England might beat the United States to claims on that part of Mexican territory.

The people in northern New Mexico did not all, by any means, welcome American control, and some plotted to recover New Mexico for the Mexicans. The plotting was centered in Taos, as usual, and as usual the New Mexicans enlisted Indian friends in their plans.

The revolt was ill-conceived and poorly-organized, and was carried out in a frenzy of resentment against arrogance and wrongs both real and fancied – a frenzy compounded by alcohol. Governer Bent and his son and others were killed, though the governor's wife and his sister-in-law, Kit Carson's wife Josefa, and others were saved. The force of the revolt soon dissipated. Its senseless savagery, acts of a few, was paid for by the death of many Indians, killed in ruthless retaliation by the United States army.

The Troubled Twenties

In 1913 the United State Supreme Court reversed a previous ruling, and held that Pueblo lands were communally owned and could not be sold by individual Indians. This stopped further alienation of Indian land, but it left in white possession a considerable acreage that had been acquired unlawfully in preceding years. Regarding the cost of this acquisition, no point was ever raised. A white economist has made a careful market analysis, and determined that $24 in goods and trinkets was a fair price for Manhattan when the whites purchased it. A dipperful of whiskey and a bit of red cloth therefore should have bought quite a lot of land in New Mexico. Of course much of the Indian land had been paid for fairly, at going land values, but from men who did not own it.

In 1920 President Harding appointed Albert B. Fall as his Secretary of the Interior. Before the Teapot Dome scandals ended his time in office, Fall joined in legislative efforts to gain for white settlers the legal title to the land acquired illegally from the Indians. The legislation introduced in Congress at Fall's instigation also threatened the remaining Indian lands and water rights.

The Indians knew little about the Fall-Bursum Bill, as the legislation was called, until in 1921 John Collier came to Taos to confer with Mabel and Tony Luhan. Then John Collier and Tony Luhan went down the line of the Pueblos telling them about the legislation. The All-Pueblo Council, forgotten for 250 years, revived, and sent a delegation to Washington to oppose the legislation, and to New York and Chicago to ask the aid of Indian friends.

The Indian Bureau was supporting the legislation, and to off-set the Indian efforts, the Bureau mounted a counter-attack against the

Pueblos. The Indian Commissioner and his Assistant Commissioner invaded the Taos Pueblo Council to accuse them of being "half animals," and "pagan worshippers." They then outlawed Indian dances and ceremonies except when held at times and under circumstances approved by the Bureau. In spite of the counter-attack, the Indians and their friends defeated the Fall-Bursum Bill in Congress, and went on to sponsor legislation for a Pueblo Lands Board to settle legal questions involving Indian lands.

The Indian Bureau's next move was to denounce the Taos Pueblo for taking boys out of school for their tribal religious training. The Taos Pueblo Council resisted, and the Bureau had all the Councilmen, the old men of the tribe, arrested and jailed in Santa Fe. The Indian Defense Association took up the Pueblo case, and the Federal District Judge released the Councilmen, rebuking the Indian Bureau and ordering them, "Take these men home."

As the Twenties ended, the Indians all over the United States had followed the Pueblos in joining together for their own betterment. A study by the Brookings Institute and the Senate Indian Committee bore out the criticisms of Indian administration by the Indians and their friends. A New Deal began in Indian affairs when in 1933 President Roosevelt appointed John Collier as Indian Commissioner.

These troubled times were not, of course, typical of the history of New Mexico, nor of the relations of the various peoples who make it up. The history we hear of, and even study in our schools, is that of conflict and crisis, rather than the less dramatic, even though "no less-renown'd," victories of peace. Troubles and difficulties there have been, and there are still more than a few. But the long history of Taos Pueblo has been in relations of friendship and mutual aid with its neighbors, and the Pueblo's present is the outgrowth of its past.

Taos Pueblo is one of New Mexico's most written of historic places, and is probably its favorite photographic subject. The only descriptive book dealing generally with Taos, however, Blanche Grant's *Taos Pueblo,* has long been out of print. The Pueblo is the locale for much of Frank Waters' highly regarded novel, *The Man Who Killed the Deer,* and of Mabel Luhan's *Winter in Taos* and *Edge of Taos Desert.*

Among the best known and most reliable of all books about Indians in general that contain information about Taos are those by John Collier and Frank Waters, published by Sage Books.

The Southwest Association on Indian Affairs, 227 Washington Ave., Santa Fe, New Mexico, is a center of helpful work among Indians, and publishes annual handbooks about Southwest Indians. The *New Mexico Magazine,* which may simply be addressed at Santa Fe, regularly carries articles and reviews about New Mexico's Indians in general and about Taos in particular.

Governor Seferino Martinez and interpreter Paul Bernal telling the Blue Lake history at a meeting of the American Association on Indian Affairs.

Ruins of the old Pueblo church destroyed by the United States Army in 1848. *Photo courtesy of the Museum of New Mexico collections.*

Taos Pueblo Fiesta in the 1880's. *Photo courtesy of Harwood Foundation Library, Taos.*

Sources of Information about Taos Pueblo

Taos Pueblo is one of America's legendary places. It has been written of in hundreds, perhaps thousands, of histories, studies, novels, stories and articles, and pictured in tens of thousands of photographs. Books and reports which provided source material for this booklet are included in the following bibliography. A few books and reports were not used because they present information harmful to Indian feelings. Information in the booklet was carefully weighed for harmony with Indian wishes, and was for the most part gained during a good many years of life in Taos and work in Indian causes.

Aberle, S.D., "The Pueblo Indians of New Mexico, Their Land, Economy and Civil Organization," Memoir No. 70, *The American Anthropologist,* Vol. 50, No. 4, Part 2.

Brayer, Herbert O., *Pueblo Indian Land Grants of the Rio Abajo,* (University of New Mexico Press, 1939).

Brown, Donald Nelson, "Taos Dance Classification," *El Palacio,* Vol. 67, No. 6.

Collier, John, *From Every Zenith* (Swallow Press, 1963).

_____ . *Indians of the Americas* (W.W. Norton & Co., 1947).

_____ . *On the Gleaming Way* (Swallow Press, 1962).

Eggan, Fred, *Social Organization of the Western Pueblos* (University of Chicago Press, 1950).

Ellis, Florence, testimony in "Petitioners Findings of Fact and Brief, Pueblo of Taos vs United States of America," Indian Claims Commission Docket No. 357.

Grant, Blanche, *Taos Indians* (Santa Fe New Mexican Publishing Co., 1925).

Hagan, William T., *American Indians* (University of Chicago Press, 1961).

Harrington, J.P., "Old Indian Geographical Names around Santa Fe, New Mexico," *The American Anthropologist,* Vol. 22, No. 4.

Herold, Laurance C. and Ralph A. Luebben, "Papers on Taos Archeology" (Fort Burgwin Research Center, 1968).

McAllester, David P., "Indian Music in the Southwest" (The Taylor Museum, 1961).

Miller, Merton L., *A Preliminary Study of the Pueblo of Taos, New Mexico* (University of Chicago Press, 1898).

Reeve, Frank D., *History of New Mexico* (Lewis Publishing Co., 1961).

Reno Philip, "Rebellion in New Mexico, 1837," *New Mexico Historical Review,* Vol. XL, No. 3.

_____ . "Tourism Possibilities for the Taos Indians," *New Mexico Business,* Vol. 19, No. 2.

Sando, Joe S., "Pueblo Indian Government History" (Mimeographed).

Waters, Frank, *Masked Gods* (Swallow Press, 1950).

_____ . "The Indian Influence on Taos Art", *New Mexico Quarterly,* Vol. XXI, No. 2.